Parental Gui

Fr eat to Driver's Seat

Don't get roped into another dull family vacation. Follow these steps and get your parents to take you to your **dream destination**.

Hang up **pictures** of the place you want to visit. When someone reads the name out loud, say, "Why, that's a **great idea**!"

Tell your parents that you're really a **visiting alien**, and they must take you to (*name of place you really want to go*) for a rendezvous with the **mothership**.

Hide the maps until everyone agrees to go where you want.

For orders other than by individual consumers, Pocket Books grants a discount on the purchase of **10 or more** copies of single titles for special markets or premium use. For further details, please write to the Vice President of Special Markets, Pocket Books, 1633 Broadway, New York, NY 10019-6785, 8th floor.

For information on how individual consumers can place orders, please write to Mail Order Dept., Simon & Schuster Inc., 200 Old Tappan Road, Old Tappan, NJ 07675.

Are We Having Fun Yet?

Summer Activities Inspired by Nickelodeon Magazine

Edited by **Carmen Morais**

Designed by **Scott Stowell**

Illustrations by **Chip Wass**

Published by POCKET BOOKS

New York London Toronto Sydney Tokyo Singapore

All That created by Brian Robbins and Mike Tollin
Kenan & Kel created by Kim Bass
Hey Arnold! created by Craig Bartlett
AAAHH!!! Real Monsters created by Klasky Csupo Inc.
The Angry Beavers created by Mitch Schauer
The Secret World of Alex Mack created by Tommy Lynch and Ken Lipman
The Mystery Files of Shelby Woo created by Alan Goodman
KABLAM! created by Will McRobb, Bob Mittenthal and Chris Viscardi
Action League Now! created by Bob Mittenthal, Will McRobb and Albie Hecht
Life With Loopy created by Stephen Holman
Henry and June created by Mark Marek
the off-beats created by Mo Willems

Photo Credits:
Stick Stickly: Roy Gumpel and Barbara Nitke; Zelda Van Gutters: Janette Beckman

A MINSTREL PAPERBACK *Original*

A Minstrel Book published by
POCKET BOOKS, a division of Simon & Schuster Inc.
1230 Avenue of the Americas, New York, NY 10020

ISBN: 0-671-01682-2

First Minstrel Books printing June 1998

10 9 8 7 6 5 4 3 2 1

Printed in the U.S.A.

Contents

Quiz: Hi, Tide *by Ted Heller*.............. **12**

Do you have a beachin' personality?

Complete-the-Rhyme:

Passport Pups *by Ted Heller*.............. **29**

Doggie doggerel

Play: Who Nose?

by Abby X. Miller and Karen Kuflik........ **36**

Stick Stickly has a nose for crime

Word Find: The State of Mings

by Ted Heller **68**

Zone in on the Ming family

Mystery: The Missing Beetle Mystery

by Richie Chevat **96**

Work with Shelby Woo

Fill-ins

by Susan Mitchell

Just add words

A (Noun) Is Born . . . **1**

A Great Place to (Verb). **54**

Dear (Parent). **93**

Greetings From (Place) **121**

Tongue Tie-ups

by Jack Krause

Twisted talk

Tongue Tie-ups. **4**

Tongue Tie-ups Two **57**

Total Tongue Tie-ups **111**

Scrambles

by Jack Krause

Turn a phrase

Pie Cop. **5**

Did I Get the Part? **22**

Lock Buns **86**

Animal Actors **87**

Goat Bin **110**

Eat These Words. . **116**

Pop Quiz
by John-Ryan Hevron
Nickelodeon trivia challenge
KABLAM! **6**
All That **20**
Hey Arnold! **34**
Kenan & Kel. **50**
AAAHH!!! Real Monsters **64**
The Secret World of Alex Mack **84**
The Angry Beavers **104**
The Mystery Files of Shelby Woo . . . **112**

Jokes
by David Lewman
We don't pull any punchlines
Jokes. **8**
More Jokes **48**
Even More Jokes . . **66**
Still More Jokes . . . **88**
Jokes Again **114**

Backyard and Backseat Business
by Jack Krause
Here's the game plan
Tag, You're Itch . . . **10**
Pelter Skelter **60**
Venus de Smile-O . . **90**

Annoying Summer Songs
by Anne D. Bernstein
You know the score
Oh, When the Ants 18
The Sunburn Song 78
Lost in the Forest 108

Check, Please
by Chris Duffy
Some looney lists
How to Tell if the Movie You're Watching Will Be the Summer's 23
Brain Drain 58
Return to Sender . . 80

Parental Guidance
by Chris Duffy
Some ifs, ands, and buts you can use
Pool for Love 52
Bedtime Bluffing . . 106

Dish It Out
by Fran Claro
Food formulas
Aquari-Yum 26
Banana Dogs 82
Green Slime Frankenstein 117

Answers 124

All activities inspired by

Fill-ins

A ______________ Is Born
(noun)

Ask a **friend** or family member to give you the words to **fill in the blanks** below. Then read this letter **out loud**.

La ______________ *Hotel*
(foreign-sounding word)

Paris, France

Dear ______________ :
(your teacher's name)

You may have heard it on the

______________, or read about it in
(noun)

the ______________________ *Times*. I won't
(your town)

be back to ______________________ this fall.
(your school)

Remember ______________________ ,
(famous basketball player)

whom we studied last year in your

______________________ ______________________
(adjective) (school subject)

class? Well, I've been picked to play the

young ______________________ 's
(same famous basketball player)

______________________ in a new made-for-
(noun)

______________________ movie! Can you
(noun)

believe it? There I was, playing

______________________ in (the) ______________________ ,
(a sport) (place)

when suddenly, someone passed me a

basketball. I ______________________ it a
(past tense verb)

bit, then made a shot. It hit the

__________________ and went in! I
(noun)

was instantly surrounded by autograph

hounds and other __________________ s.
(kind of dog)

Next thing I knew, I was given a(n)

______________ ______________ to
(adjective) (noun)

sign and flown to Paris. Filming starts

in a few days. And it looks like I won't

be back in ________________ until
(your town)

________________ . Oh well!
(last day of school)

I hope you won't miss me too much.

Your faithful student,

____
(your name)

Tongue Tie-ups

Can you say these

tongue twisters ten times, fast?

Sneaking in my creaky squeaky reeking summer sneakers.

Why is Wyatt roasting wieners when Wendy and Brett bought bratwurst?

Bee stings sting severely when it's sunburned skin that's stung.

I'm hooked on the book Brooke brought back from the brook-side bookstore.

Pie Cop

Unscramble the words below to spell out the names of summertime **drinks** and **foods**. We did the first one for you. **Answers on p. 124.**

pie cop i c e p o p

eat dice ___ ___ ___ ___   ___ ___ ___

her best ___ ___ ___ ___ ___ ___ ___

lone dame ___ ___ ___ ___ ___ ___ ___ ___

race mice ___ ___ ___   ___ ___ ___ ___ ___

raging eel ___ ___ ___ ___ ___ ___   ___ ___ ___

hi to some ___ ___ ___ ___ ___ ___ ___ ___

Pop Quiz

How **well** do you know Nickelodeon's *KABLAM!*™?
Take this **trivia test** and find out. Circle true or false next to each statement below. **Answers on p. 124.**

Action League Now!

T F 1. The Flesh is super-strong—and super-naked.

T F 2. Meltman has the power to melt cars.

T F 3. In one episode, Bill the Lab Guy's daughter is kidnapped by a giant baby.

T F 4. Thundergirl is an alien from the Reticulon Galaxy.

Life With Loopy

T F 5. Loopy is a droopy-eared basset hound.

T F 6. Loopy once tries to become more beautiful by zipping herself into a cocoon for a week.

T F 7. Twelve-year-old Larry is Loopy's younger brother.

T F 8. The only thing that calms Loopy down is mint ice cream.

Henry and June

T F 9. "KABLAM!" is the sound made when June starts a new cartoon.

T F 10. Henry was once temporarily replaced by another host named Hector.

T F 11. September from *the off-beats* is June's brother.

T F 12. Henry and June live in a comic book.

T F 13. Henry's dream is to co-star in a comic book with Aquaman.

Jokes

What does Krumm like to ride in the summer?

A bicycle built for boo.

❋

What does Winnie like to ride in the summer?

A bicycle built for Pooh.

❋

What does Heffer like to ride in the summer?

A bicycle built for moo.

What has four wheels and grows on a vine?

A skategourd.

❋

Why do scientists like baseball?

Because they love looking at slides.

How did the pig do at bat?

He hit a ham run.

Where do pitchers learn new pitches?

In the enstrikelopedia.

When do ballplayers get emotional?

When they choke up at bat.

What did the termite say to his friend at the baseball diamond?

"Let's get a bat to eat."

Why did the baseball player take his bat to the library?

Because his teacher told him to hit the books.

Backyard Business

Tag, You're Itch!

Backyards are **full of things** that make you itchy: cut grass, mosquitoes, **fleas**. In this game, called **Itch Tag**, there's a new itchy thing in your yard. See if you can escape without a scratch.

What You Need:

- At least three **people**

Setup:

- **Choose one person** to be "Itch."
- Figure out a home base, called **Calamine Island**.

How to Play:

- One player, called **Itch** (not It), tries to tag someone to make the other person become Itch. Everyone else tries to keep from getting tagged. If you're being chased by Itch, there are three things you can do:
  1. **Run** like mad.
  2. Squat and yell out a summertime itch, such as "poison ivy," "mosquito bite," or "**wet sand in my bathing suit**." Itch must leave you alone if you say one of these phrases. You can use this trick only once.
  3. Hide in Calamine Island, where you **can't be tagged**. If Itch finds you there, however, Itch can call out "One scratch, two scratch, three scratch, run!" and then you must leave. If you don't, the game **stops**, and you automatically become Itch.
- If Itch touches you, you have been **infected**. The game stops, and you become the new Itch.

Hi, Tide

Most people **like** to spend the summer at the **shore**. Do you? Take our quiz and see if a **day at the beach** would be a real **day at the beach** for you.

1. When you're swimming in the ocean and you see a fin, you should assume:
    a. **there is a shark connected to it**
    b. **someone is wearing a very pointy swimcap**
    c. **a fin time will be had by all**

2. You think the white stuff on the lifeguard's nose is:
    a. **the lifeguard's nose**
    b. **just to impress girls**
    c. **zinc oxide, which protects against sunburn**

3. Sand is:
    a. **dandruff from clouds**
    b. **tiny grains of disintegrated rock**
    c. **snow that has been baked by the sun**

4. When someone yells, "Surf's up!" you think:
   a. **somebody is surfing the Internet**
   b. **someone just upchucked the surf 'n' turf special**
   c. **the waves are good for surfing**

5. You should avoid jellyfish because they:
   a. **don't taste as good as jamfish**
   b. **are just plain ugly and creepy**
   c. **might sting you**

6. A *beachcomber* is:
   a. **a person who runs a comb through the beach to get all the tangles out of the sand**
   b. **a person who searches the beach for shells or interesting debris**
   c. **a rare piece of flat, plastic driftwood that has a row of long, thin teeth**

7. When a lifeguard whistles and waves her hands, it means:

a. **swimmers have drifted out of the designated swimming area**

b. **she's had it with being a lifeguard; she's practicing to be a basketball guard**

c. **everybody in the water should do the wave**

8. Mouth-to-mouth resuscitation should be given to:

a. **a beached whale**

b. **a swimmer who has nearly drowned**

c. **anyone you feel like**

9. When you hear someone say "high tide" you:

a. **know that's when the water comes up higher on the shore**

b. **wonder if there's a medium tide**

c. **hope the tide says "hi" back**

10. The Sandman is:

a. **a mythical genie that puts you to sleep**

b. **the guy who delivers the sand to the beach every morning**

c. **your nickname**

Now add up your points:

1. a = 3, b = 2, c = 1.
2. a = 1, b = 2, c = 3.
3. a = 2, b = 3, c = 1.
4. a = 1, b = 2, c = 3.
5. a = 1, b = 2, c = 3.
6. a = 2, b = 3, c = 1.
7. a = 3, b = 1, c = 2.
8. a = 2, b = 3, c = 1.
9. a = 3, b = 2, c = 1.
10. a = 3, b = 1, c = 2.

Shore Score

- 24 to 30 points: **Beach Bum**.

  You were born with sand in your hair.
- 17 to 23 points: **SPF 30**.

  Hit the beach, but not too hard.
- 10 to 16 points: **Sand Crab**.

  You'd rather be camping.

Oh, When the Ants

(Sing to the tune of
"When the Saints Go Marching In.")

Oh, when the **ants**
Get in our food,
It puts us in an awful mood.
We find legs in our egg salad,
When the ants get in our food.

Oh, when the **dog**
Drools on our meal,
To eat at all loses appeal.
We find slobber on our sandwich,
When the dog drools on our meal.

Oh, when the **sand**
Gets in our lunch,
Potato chips have extra crunch.
We find grit in ground-beef patties,
When the sand gets in our lunch.

Oh, when the **flies**
Land on our spread,
We've no desire to be fed.
We find bugs on our bologna,
When the flies land on our spread.

Next time we **dine**
We'll stay inside.
Our hungry mouths we'll open wide.
Within walls, it's safe to swallow.
Next time we dine we'll stay inside.

Pop Quiz

How **well** do you know Nickelodeon's *All That*™? Take this **trivia test** and find out. Circle the correct answer for each question below. **Answers on p. 124.**

1. Where is Ishboo from?

   a. **a foreign land**
   b. **Seattle**
   c. **Steak City**

2. Who is Earboy's best friend?

   a. **Dirt Breath**
   b. **Pizza Face**
   c. **Chicken Boy**

3. Chef Randy is obsessed with:

   a. **chocolate**
   b. **grilled cheese**
   c. **ketchup**

4. What is Superdude's only weakness?

a. **lactose intolerance**

b. **claustrophobia**

c. **nacho chips**

5. What is the name of the character Josh Server plays in the band Bacteria?

a. **Larvae**

c. **Maggot**

b. **Grime**

6. Larisa Oleynik, who plays Alex Mack on *The Secret World of Alex Mack*, once played a character on *All That* called:

a. **Relaxed Mack**

b. **Alex Sax**

c. **Malix Ack**

7. What character has appeared the most times on the show?

a. **Mrs. Fingerley**

c. **Chef Farley**

b. **Randy**

Scrambles

Did I Get the Part?

Each of the phrases below about a **body part** is made up of letters from a celebrity's name. Can you **unscramble** the phrases so they correctly complete each star's name? We did the first one for you. **Answers on p. 124.**

~~knees~~	**leg hop**	**liver stone**
	eyes	**music toe**

K **E** A **N** U R **E** E V E **S**

M I K _ M _ _ R _

O _ _ _ _ _ _ _ _ _ _

W _ _ O _ I G O _ D B _ R _

_ _ _ _ R _ _ _ _

Use this **check-list** to figure out if the best thing about the film you're seeing is the acting and plot—or the **air-conditioning and popcorn**.

How to Tell if the Movie You're Watching Will Be the Summer's...

. . . Biggest Blockbuster

___ There are more **explosions** in it than there are hairs on your head.

___ The bad guy has stolen a nuclear weapon—and there's only **this one guy in the whole world** who can stop him.

___ The main character is an **alien-superhero-vampire-spy**.

___ You already know all the words to the pop song played during the **credits**.

___ The actors have **dollar signs** in their eyes.

___ The hero can't act, but, boy, can he **kickbox**!

. . . Or Biggest Bomb

___ The villain is about as scary as **Elmo**.

___ The audience shouts to **turn the lights on**.

___ You find yourself carefully examining the **hair** of the person in front of you.

___ The characters keep saying "**I can't believe it**" and neither can you.

___ The last time you had this little fun was at the **dentist**.

___ Your parents' video of your **third birthday** had more action.

___ The hero can act, but, boy, he can't **kickbox** at all!

Dish It Out

Aquari-Yum

Next time your mom gets on your case to eat **fish**, tell her you have just the recipe in mind . . . then show her **this one**.

What You Need:

- 1 **adult** (to help)
- 1 package **flavored blue gelatin**
- 20 or more **gummi fish** (you can also use gummi worms)
- 1 can of **whipped cream**

- 1 large, clear glass or plastic bowl, or a brand new, **well-washed** small fishbowl
- Clear, short **drinking glasses** or small, glass dessert dishes

What To Do:

1. Ask an adult to help you prepare the package of blue gelatin, according to the **directions** on the box.
2. Put 2 cups of the blue gelatin liquid in a small bowl, and place it in the **refrigerator** to set. You will use this later to make choppy ocean waves.
3. Fill the large bowl or fishbowl with the rest of the gelatin. This will be your aquarium. **Set it aside** for a few minutes, until the gelatin starts to thicken a bit.
4. Stick **18 gummi fish** into the blue gelatin, so they look like they're swimming in it.

5. Put the large bowl in the refrigerator, until the gelatin **sets** completely.
6. When the gelatin has set, take both bowls **out of the refrigerator**.
7. Use a spoon to **chop up** the gelatin in the small bowl.
8. Add the blue chunks to your aquarium, so they look like **choppy ocean waves**.
9. Spray whipped cream on the waves, as if it were **sea foam**.
10. Wedge 1 or 2 gummi fish into the chunks to look as if they're **leaping** out of the water.
11. Admire your aquarium, but **don't feed the fish**. Spoon the sweet seafood into dessert dishes or glasses, and **feed your face** instead.

Passport Pups

Zelda Van Gutters, *Nickelodeon Magazine*'s **Roving Reporter**, and the poet **Rufus FitzPumpkin**, her Irish Setter boyfriend, took a trip **around the world**. On the next page is Rufus's poem about their adventure, but the last word in each stanza is missing. Can you **complete the rhyme**? The missing word in each stanza rhymes with the second line in that stanza. We've done the first one for you. **Answers on p. 124.**

And boy, are my paws tired.

Zelda

Of our summer vacation
I'll now wag a **tale**.
To roam the world was our plan,
and soon we set s a i l.

First to Washington, D.C.
And the Capitol's **dome**.
When we barked at the White House,
Socks the cat was not h ___ ___ ___.

Next, with crowds in Times Square,
We both had to **grapple**.
That's the core of the problem,
In New York, the Big A ___ ___ ___ ___.

On a hot Miami beach
I saw old folks play **bingo**.
Zelly swam with a bird,
Some tall pink f ___ ___ ___ ___ ___ ___ ___.

Next we flew down to Chile.
Where we two furry **dandies**
Saw penguins near the South Pole,
And llamas in the A ___ ___ ___ ___.

And then in the Amazon,
A monkey was our **waiter**
At this rainforest restaurant
Which was on the

e ___ ___ ___ ___ ___ ___.

We spent two weeks in Paris,
Never once a rain **shower**.
Burned our poor shoeless paws,
Climbing the Eiffel T ___ ___ ___ ___.

We then cooled off in Venice
In water dark just like **cola**,
But got two traffic tickets
When we crashed our g ___ ___ ___ ___ ___ ___ .

From there we went to Egypt.
The first thing Zel and I **did**
Was rush off to the desert
To see the Great
P___ ___ ___ ___ ___ ___ .

When we landed in Kenya
Zelly was really **sorry**
She'd forgotten the film
For our African s ___ ___ ___ ___ ___ .

While we were in India
We ate food made with **curry**
Which made us feel extra hot
Since we're
already so f ___ ___ ___ ___.

Then to Japan we traveled.
Where some little kid we **met**
Thought I had a reset button,
Thought I was a virtual p ___ ___.

Last of all, a policeman
Said "I might have to **fine ya**,"
When he saw me lift one leg
Near the Great Wall of C ___ ___ ___ ___.

From Asia to Africa
To England's white cliffs of **Dover**,
We've loved traveling the world,
Now our vacation's o ___ ___ ___ .

How **well** do you know Nickelodeon's *Hey Arnold!*™? Take this **trivia test** and find out. Circle true or false next to each statement below. **Answers on p. 125.**

T F 1. Arnold's real first name is Hey.

T F 2. *Hey Arnold!* takes place in New York City.

T F 3. Arnold's principal's name is Mr. Wartz.

T F 4. Gerald is an only child.

T F 5. Grandma was a librarian in her youth.

T F 6. Helga's secret shrine to Arnold includes an aluminum-foil bust of him.

T F 7. Arnold's grandparents run a bakery.

T F 8. Helga hates the fact that she is secretly in love with Arnold.

T F 9. After Eugene, the kid who always has bad luck, watches his bike get run over, Arnold welds it back together.

T F 10. Helga calls Arnold "basketball head."

T F 11. Arnold's favorite music is jazz.

T F 12. Stoop Kid is Arnold's older brother.

T F 13. Helga once lost a spelling bee on purpose, to get back at her dad.

T F 14. After catching Mickey Kaline's home-run baseball, Arnold sells it for $400.

T F 15. Arnold and his grandmother once saved an abused tortoise from the city aquarium.

Who Nose?

Are you **stuck** on Stick Stickly, the wooden host of *Nick in the Afternoon*? Then you and up to three of your friends can put on this **Stick Stickly play**. Make the characters out of **ice-pop sticks** and act out the skit, or just read it aloud.

The Cast:

- **Stick Stickly**
- **Wood Knot**—a stand-up comedian and Stick's twin brother
- **Dr. Schnoz**—an evil nose-snatching villain who has no nose of his own
- **Boogie Boy**—Dr. Schnoz's sidekick. He talks as if he has the sniffles.

What You Need:

- 4 **ice-pop sticks**
- Stuff to **decorate** the sticks with, such as markers, construction paper, beads, glitter, plastic **eyes**, clay, yarn, cotton balls, glue, **anything you want**
- 1 small, real **leaf** from a tree
- 1 Stick-size **pie, bottle, and garbage can**. (You can make them out of construction paper or clay.)

continued

What to Do:

- Turn the ice-pop sticks into the characters. Stick Stickly and Wood Knot are identical twins, so they should look the same. You can make up what the other characters look like.
- Stick's nose should be able to come off his face easily. Don't give Dr. Schnoz a nose; he doesn't have one.

When you're ready, the play starts on the next page.

Inside Dr. Schnoz's hideout.

Dr. Schnoz: I'm finished, BB. I'm through. I'll never find the perfect nose. Never. Never!

Boogie Boy: *(Sniff)* But Boss, what about the batch you snatched today? You must have stolen ten or twenty noses!

Dr. Schnoz: Worthless. Not a usable nose in the bunch. Some were too big. Some were too long. And some of them never stopped running. They were all unacceptable . . . and *messy*!

Boogie Boy: Oh, Boss, *(Sniff)* it's not that bad.

Dr. Schnoz: That's easy for you to say, BB. You were born with a nose. All your life you've smelled fresh baked cookies, spring flowers, sweaty sneakers. *(Starts crying. He hears Stick on TV and looks at the screen.)* Wait! *(He stops crying.)* Wait! Who's that?

Boogie Boy: Why, Boss, that's Stick Stickly. Everybody knows Stick.

Dr. Schnoz: Look at that nose. So shapely, so yellow, so *sassy*! It's . . . perfect!

Boogie Boy: Oh no, Boss. You're not going to . . .

Dr. Schnoz: Oh yes, Boogie Boy. I am. All my life I've been waiting for the chance to pick my nose—and that's the one!

At the park, in the afternoon. Dr. Schnoz and Boogie Boy are secretly trailing Stick.

Stick: Ah, what a beautiful day! I feel fantastic. I feel stupendous. I feel like dancing! *(Starts dancing.)* Oh, yeah, watch my moves. . . . Go, Stick . . .

Dr. Schnoz: *(Whispers to Boogie Boy.)* Look—there he is, BB. If only I could figure out a way to get to his nose without him noticing.

(Dr. Schnoz and Boogie Boy keep watching Stick dance. Suddenly, Stick trips and falls.)

Stick: Whoooooaaaaaaa! *(Stick is knocked out. Dr. Schnoz and Boogie Boy run up to him.)*

Boogie Boy: He's out cold, Boss. *(Sniff)*

Dr. Schnoz: That's fantastic!

Boogie Boy: I think it's terrible. *(Sniff)* Are you *really* sure you want to do this?

Dr. Schnoz: Abso-posi-*schnozi*-lutely! Quick, BB. Grab the nose . . . and let's blow!

(Boogie Boy yanks off Stick's nose and runs away with the doctor. Seconds later, Stick wakes up.)

Stick: Huh? What just happened? I must have fallen or something. *(Stick gets up, walks out of the park, and down the street. He looks at his reflection in a store window and sees he has no nose.)* Ah! My nose! It's gone! My little yellow honker! Missing! Ahhhhhhhh! *(Runs home.)*

Stick's house, a few minutes later. Stick bursts in. He has no nose.

Stick: *(Frantically)* Mom! Mom! Come quick! You'll never believe it!

Wood Knot: Mom is at water aerobics, bro. Hey! What happened to you? Cat got your nose? Ha!

Stick: I don't know what happened. One minute I was dancing, the next—I was de-nosed!

Wood Knot: Looks like the work of the evil Dr. Schnoz, the nastiest nose-nabber of them all.

Stick: Oh, brother! Simmerdown, Stick. Anyhoo, why did he have to take *my* nose?

Wood Knot: Come on, bro. You have a bee-*you*-tee-full nose, if I do say so myself! But don't worry. We'll get your nose back.

Stick: We will? How?

Wood Knot: We'll just offer a reward for your little honker. A reward always works!

Stick: Great idea! How much money do you have?

Wood Knot: Me? I'm broke. How about you?

Stick: I got $3.73.

Wood Knot: Uh, forget the reward—how about some pizza instead? Two slices, comin' up!

Stick: Wood Knot! How can you talk about pizza at a time like this? I can't smell or taste a thing without my nose. I'm really—Wait a minute. . . . That's it! Wood Knot, are you thinking what I'm thinking?

Wood Knot: Pepperoni?

Stick: No. If Dr. Schnoz has my nose, then he loves the smells that I love. And what smell do I love the best?

Wood Knot: Mom's perfume?

Stick: No.

Wood Knot: Fish sticks?

Stick: No. I love the smell of Grannie Stickly's double-dutch brownie-bottomed crackleberry pie!

Wood Knot: That was my next guess. Honest!

Stick: Quick! Let's go bake a double-dutch brownie-bottomed crackleberry pie. Dr. Schnoz won't be able to resist the smell. He'll come right here to the house, and I can get my nose back!

Wood Knot: Good thinking . . . but do we still have time to grab a slice?

Outside Stick's house, later that day. The pie is sitting on a window ledge. Dr. Schnoz and Boogie Boy walk up to it.

Dr. Schnoz: I've never smelled anything so incredible in my whole life.

Boogie Boy: *(Sniff)* I thought you never smelled anything in your whole life.

Dr. Schnoz: Good point! But this aroma . . . it's so sweet, so lovely. What is it?

Boogie Boy: Looks like a double-dutch *(Sniff)* brownie-bottomed *(Sniff)* crackleberry pie.

Dr. Schnoz: I think I'm in love.

(Dr. Schnoz stuffs the whole pie in his mouth, then passes out. Stick and Wood Knot come running up. Boogie Boy sees them, but runs behind a tree before they notice him.)

Stick: It worked! Now grab my nose!

Wood Knot: Don't worry, Stick. I *nose* what I'm doing. Ha! *(Tries to pull Stick's nose off Dr. Schnoz.)* Oh, I can't! It's stuck. He must have used some sort of Hibiscus Proboscis Epoxy.

Stick: What?

Wood Knot: Nose glue.

Stick: Oh no! Now what are we going to do?

(Boogie Boy walks up, hiding his face behind a leaf. He hands Stick a bottle.)

Boogie Boy: Here, Stick. Try this. *(Runs away.)*

Stick: Huh?

Wood Knot: Hey, look at the label. This is Hibiscus Proboscis Anti-epoxy Poxy!

Stick: What?

Wood Knot: Nose-glue remover!

Stick: Oh, quick, pour it on!

(Wood Knot applies the glue remover. Stick plucks his nose off Dr. Schnoz's face. He and Wood Knot then drag the noseless Dr. Schnoz into a garbage can.)

Inside Stick's house, later that day. Stick's nose is on his face again.

Wood Knot: Now that you got your perky yellow honker back, let's go and get ourselves a big ol' pepperoni pizza-rific pie.

Stick: Good idea, Wood Knot. I can already smell it.

Wood Knot: Great! You still have that $3.73, so you can pay for it.

Stick: Oh, brother! Okay. Hey, Wood Knot, I was thinking. . . .

Wood Knot: About getting chocolate ice cream with potato chips for dessert?

Stick: No. Who was that little guy who gave us the nose-glue remover?

Wood Knot: Who nose, my friend. Who nose!

The End

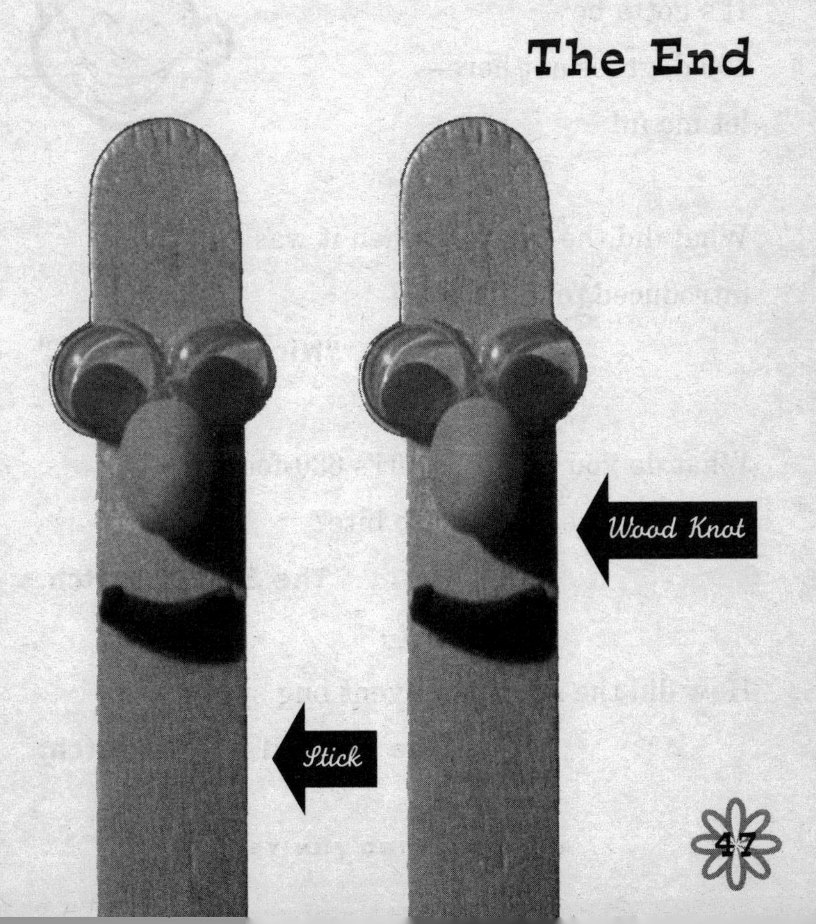

More Jokes

Knock, knock.

Who's there?

Scott.

Scott who?

It's gotta be
100 degrees out here—
let me in!

What did the Sun say when it was introduced to the Earth?

"Nice to heat you."

What do you call Missouri's 630-foot monument to a mosquito bite?

The St. Louis Itch.

How did the scientist invent bug spray?

She started from scratch.

Which movie director always
forgets to wear sunblock?

Steven Peelberg.

What do you call the Backstreet Boys
when it's 100 degrees out?

A sweat band.

What do you call a bunny with skinned knees?

A scabbit.

What's the magic word for getting rid of scabs?

Scabracadabra.

Does it work?

Scabsolutely!

Pop Quiz

How **well** do you know Nickelodeon's *Kenan & Kel*™? Take this **trivia test** and find out. Circle the correct answer for each question below. **Answers on p. 125.**

1. *Kenan & Kel* takes place in what city?

   a. **Toronto**
   b. **Orlando**
   c. **Chicago**

2. Where does Kenan Rockmore work?

   a. **Rigby's**
   b. **Taco Emporium**
   c. **Good Burger**

3. What is Kel Kimble's favorite drink?

a. **chocolate milk**　　c. **iced tea**

b. **orange soda**

4. What does Kenan do to earn extra money to buy a mountain bike?

a. **He plays Santa Claus at the mall.**

b. **He works as Kel's butler for a week.**

c. **He wins a beauty contest.**

5. What do Kenan and Kel do with the sixty-four million dollars they win in the lottery?

a. **They donate it to an orphanage.**

b. **They buy and then quickly lose a candy bar factory.**

c. **Nothing, because they lose the lottery ticket and can't collect the prize.**

6. Who sings the *Kenan & Kel* theme song?

a. **Will Smith**　　c. **Jewel**

b. **Coolio**

Parental Guidance

Pool for Love

Don't spend another summer playing in the sprinkler. Follow these steps to convince your parents to get a **giant in-ground pool**.

Buy a lot of **pool toys**, put them in the back-yard, and say, "Don't they look so sad?"

Tell everyone your doctor said you have a rare medical condition and must **soak in huge amounts of water** twice a day.

Refer to the garden as "the **deep end**."

Casually mention positive-sounding facts, such as "Did you know that Bill Gates, Julius Caesar, and George Washington attribute their success to early exposure to **chlorine**?"

Bring home a note from school saying "(*your name*) will fail my class unless he/she spends more time studying **large swimming pools**."

Do the **backstroke** from room to room.

Leave phony messages on the answering machine from the national **swim team** saying they're coming over.

Fill-ins

A Great Place to ____________
(verb)

Ask a **friend** or family member to give you the words to **fill in the blanks** below. Then read this letter **out loud**.

Dear ____________________,
(your friend's name)

Today was definitely the best day of our trip so far. We went to the All-Star

__________________ Cafe for my
(animal)

birthday, and I am still __________________!
(-ing verb)

When I first walked into the Cafe, I

couldn't believe my ________________ s. The
(body part)

food is served by *real* ________________ s!
(same animal)

I didn't know what to order, so my

mother convinced me to get this awesome

__________________ , which tasted just
(food)

like a(n) __________________. Even my
(noun)

father was impressed—he said his dinner

was fit for a __________________.
(noun)

After we ate, the entire wait staff

gathered around our __________________
(noun)

and sang "________________ Birthday" to
(adjective)

me. Then they brought out a piece of cake

with a ________________ on top.
(noun)

It was a great birthday dinner and the

most ________________ eating
(adjective)

experience of my entire life. I'll never be

able to go back to ________________
(adjective)

cafeteria food again!

Signed,

____
(your name)

Tongue Tie-ups Two

Can you say these **tongue twisters** ten times, fast?

Kent sent Trent the rent to rent Trent's tent.

Sally saw Shelley singing swinging summer swimming songs.

The corn on the cob made Bob the Slob's sobbing stop.

The ocean sure soaked Sherman.

Check, Please

Brain Drain

How to Tell You Need a Vacation

If you can check off more than **four** of these sentences, it's time for you to **swap the three R's*** for **some R & R****.

__ You're starting to like the **smell of chalk**.

__ You **pledge allegiance** to the flag before going to bed.

___On weekends, you ask your parents, "When's **recess**?"

___A local university wants to start an **archaeological dig** in your locker.

___You carry a sharpened **number-two pencil** everywhere you go.

___You've **memorized** all of your teacher's outfits.

___Your seat on the school bus has molded itself to the shape of your **bottom**.

* Reading, Writing, and 'Rithmetic

** Rest and Relaxation

Backyard Business

Pelter Skelter

If you think **dodging water balloons** sounds like a great way to **dodge the heat** on a sweltering summer day, then you're ready for a game of Pelter Skelter. Find some **friends**, put on some **beach clothes**, and you'll be **hopping wet** in no time.

What You Need:

- At least three **people**
- At least ten **water balloons**
- Clothes you can get **wet** in

Setup:

- Choose one person to be the "**Pelter**."
- Everyone else is called a "**Hopper**."
- Establish an **imaginary straight line** on the playing field. The Pelter won't be able to cross that line.
- Make a "Pelter Shelter" area several feet away from the line. This is the Hoppers' **home base**.

How to Play:

1. The Hoppers **stand in a row** on the line, facing the Pelter Shelter. The Pelter stands behind the Hoppers like a football quarter-back, and puts two water balloons on the ground at his or her feet.
2. When everyone is ready, the Pelter picks up one water balloon, tosses it **straight up in the air**, and yells, "Pelter Skelter! Run for shelter!"

continued

3. As soon as the Pelter begins the shout, all the Hoppers start **hopping** on one leg toward the Pelter Shelter. The Pelter then catches the water balloon and tosses it at the Hoppers, but the Pelter cannot cross the line and chase them.
4. The Hoppers cannot catch the balloon. They must **dodge** it. Any Hoppers who get hit with the water balloon are out. All Hoppers who make it to the Pelter Shelter are safe for the rest of the round.
5. When the first balloon has been tossed, the Pelter picks up the other water balloon, throws it straight up and **again** shouts, "Pelter Skelter! Run for shelter!"
6. The round is over when the second balloon has been tossed at the Hoppers. The first person to make it to the Pelter Shelter without getting hit becomes the next **Pelter**.

7. A new round begins with a new Pelter and two new water balloons. **Keep playing** until all the balloons have been used up.

Penalties Box

- If the water balloon **bursts** all over the Pelter, the Pelter is out. The person who was the Pelter last becomes the Pelter again. If this happens when you first start playing, then choose someone else to be the new Pelter.
- If the Pelter crosses the line, the round **ends** and the person who was the Pelter last becomes the Pelter again.

Pop Quiz

How **well** do you know Nickelodeon's *AAAHH!!! Real Monsters*™? Take this **trivia test** and find out. Circle true or false next to each statement below. **Answers on p. 125.**

T F 1. Monsters use toenail clippings for money.

T F 2. Ickis's father, Sickis, flunked out of the Monster Academy.

T F 3. Oblina always complains that Krumm spends too much time in the shower.

T F 4. The monsters' teacher, the Gromble, loves to wear bright green high-heeled shoes.

T F 5. The Snorch is able to speak directly to the other monsters for the first time after getting the CUTT-3000 voice box implanted in his throat.

T F 6. During the Festival of the Festering Moon, all adolescent monsters shed their skin.

T F 7. Krumm likes to scare humans by pulling out his eyeballs.

T F 8. Simon the Monster Hunter's ultimate monster-hunting machine looks just like a school bus.

T F 9. When Ickis really wants to scare someone, his eyes turn red, and he grows.

T F 10. Monsters are not allowed to watch human television shows or movies.

Even More Jokes

What kind of hair does the ocean have?

Wavy.

Which waves are impossible to swim in?

Microwaves.

Why did the kid eat a handful of sand?

He wanted to grit his teeth.

Which rock band loves to throw
gourds in a pool?

Splashing Pumpkins.

What do you call 90 musicians in the pool?

A swimphony orchestra.

What class teaches you how to jump off the high board?

Diver's Education.

Where do they teach it?

Boarding school.

What did the ocean say to the shore?

"Am I glad to sea you!"

What did the kid's friends say after she visited the ocean?

"You look like you've seen a coast."

Why do oceans never go out of style?

Because they're always current.

The State of Mings

In the following tale, Al and Ma Ming and their five kids (Phil, Mary, Ken, Carol, and Mindi) can't decide where to spend their **summer vacation**. Hidden in the story, meanwhile, are the names of **thirty-nine of the United States**. Can you find them all? (Hint: Punctuation and spaces between words don't count, and neither do capital letters.) The first state has been underlined for you. **Answers on pgs. 125-127.**

Here's a list of the states in the order they appear in the story:

Ohio, Texas, Washington, Iowa, Indiana, Alaska, Utah, New Jersey, Montana, Florida, Kentucky, Louisiana, Arizona, Virginia, West Virginia, Missouri, North Carolina, South Carolina, Arkansas, Kansas, Mississippi, Maine, Idaho, Maryland, North Dakota, South Dakota, Alabama, Colorado, New York, Vermont, Georgia, Rhode Island, Tennessee, Minnesota, Nevada, Illinois, New Mexico, Wisconsin, Wyoming

The Ming family was sitting in the dining room, listening to the radio and talking about their summer vacation.

"Although I'd love to go to that Civil War battle town, Shiloh, I ought to spend the money on a new Gore-Tex jacket instead," said Al Ming from behind his newspaper.

"Don't use the Gore-Tex as an excuse," his wife, Ma Ming, said. "I'm already washing tons of Gore-Tex jackets you've bought. You don't need another."

Mary, their twenty-year-old daughter, poked her head in from the kitchen. "I can't handle that radio wailing anymore. Turn it off, Phil!" she yelled to her older brother, then went back to the kitchen.

"Do any of you know what's bothering Mary?" Ma asked.

"I do," said eleven-year-old Mindi, an A student in school. "We were at a gala skating party last night, and Mary slipped and fell. She's been

in a rut, a huge rut, ever since. I'll go see if she's alright." Mindi got up and left the room.

A few minutes later, Mary walked in. "I'm sorry I snapped at you, Phil," she said. "I've been upset since I ruined my new jersey while skating yesterday."

"That's okay," said Phil.

"Time to eat," said Mindi, walking in to the room with a big bowl of salad. "I tried to make the salad really colorful. I put in orange carrots, a yellow lemon, tan almonds, and green peppers."

"That salad is looking really florid, as usual, Min," Phil said.

Carol and Ken, Al and Ma Ming's teenaged kids, walked in, followed by Dako, the family's golden retriever.

"Ken, tuck your shirt in, dear," Ma said.

"Carol, did you sell your car to that guy Lou today?" asked Al.

"No," Carol answered. "I don't know where

Lou is. I analyzed his offer to buy my Ferrari Z on an installment plan, but he hasn't called me back yet."

"Maybe he's on vacation," Ken said.

"Speaking of vacation, where should we go this summer?" asked Ma.

"How about going east?" Ken suggested, as he piled salad on his plate. "We could fly on that airline—Virgin. I always hear good things about them."

"I am *not* flying," Carol interrupted. "East or west. Virgin! I am afraid of flying and you know it, Ken. Besides, we can't take Dako on a plane. Wouldn't you guys miss our incredibly cute little Dako?" Carol reached her hand out and petted the loyal pup.

"Okay, okay," Ken answered. "We could go north. Carol in a car with Dako and the rest of us in a plane."

"No," Phil said, "Let's go south, Carol in a car with Dako and us in a plane."

"On the other hand, it's always been my dream to fly to Sweden!" Carol suddenly suggested, surprising everyone at the table. Even Dako let out a bark. "An S.A.S. plane flies there every day. Get ready for a shock—an S.A.S. plane I might actually get on!" Carol laughed.

"But, Carol," said Mindi, "I thought you were afraid to fly."

"I am, but going to Sweden is a trip I wouldn't miss," Carol said.

"Well," Ken replied, "going to England is a trip *I* wouldn't miss. Is sipping tea in London something you'd like to do, too, Ma?"

"I can picture Ma in England," Mary said.

"Actually, I'd prefer to go to Los Angeles," Ma Ming confessed.

"Sorry, but I don't think we can go to London or Los Angeles," Al said. "A hotel room in either city would be too expensive."

"So maybe we should just buy a hotel for our very own!" Mary joked.

Al thought for a minute and said, "I think you're on to something, Mary. Land is a wise investment. Maybe we should forget our vacation and buy some property instead."

"I was only kidding, Dad!" Mary said. "Seriously, this year, I'd like us to head north—Dako! Take your paws off my pants! What's gotten into you?" she asked the pup.

Phil said, "No, I think we should go south. . . . Dako! Take your paws off Mary's pants."

"Didn't you just hear that loud *bam* outside?" said Al. "A *bam* always gets Dako upset. Come here, boy." The dog trotted over to Al, curled up at his feet and went to sleep.

Ken, who was now reading the newspaper, put a color ad on the table and said, "Here's something new. Yo, RKO just opened a new theater near my friend Monty's house. Let's spend our vacation just going to the movies!"

"Yeah! Let's go tonight!" said Mindi.

"After dinner we can drive over. Monty's

always up for a movie," Ken replied.

"I was at that new theater last weekend," said Carol. "It's huge. Even the popcorn comes in large, extra large, or giant size. Achoo!"

"Gesundheit," said Ken. "You've been sneezing a lot lately, Carol. Maybe you have catarrh. That's what you call an inflammation of a mucus membrane, you know. I read a poem about it somewhere."

Carol became very annoyed. "Ken, I wrote the poem you're talking about! My "Catarrh Ode" is landing in every poetry magazine in the country! How could you forget?"

"I'm sorry, Carol," Ken said.

"I didn't know you were capable of such rottenness. Eesh!" Carol said.

"That's enough, you two," said Al. Just then, the doorbell rang. "Can you get it, Min? Nesota, the guy from next door, said he'd stop by."

Mindi went to the door and came back with the Mings' neighbors, Eva and Xavier Nesota.

"Come in, Eva, darling, and Xavier," said Ma.

Xavier Nesota barged into the room. "Hello, everyone! Say, are you guys ill? I noisily banged on the door and no one answered."

"Sorry," replied Phil. "We didn't hear you."

"Hey, X," said Al suddenly to his neighbor. "I saw you at the grocery store today. You acted as if you hardly knew me, X. I couldn't believe it!"

"That wasn't me," Xavier said. "That must have been my twin brother, Constantino."

"You have a twin brother?" asked Ken.

"Yes, he's visiting me for the weekend. Con is a singer at a beach resort," said Xavier.

"Wow! Is Con singing at that brand new resort down south?" Phil asked.

"Yes," said Xavier. "Do you know it?"

"I heard it's great," said Ma Ming.

"Yeah," said Mindi. "Really great."

"Well, Con says it's fantastic," said Xavier. "We're going there for our vacation. He's getting us a discount on the room."

The Ming family's faces lit up. "Say, X," asked Al, "do you think Con could get us some rooms, too?"

Xavier's eyes got all dewy. "O Ming family, that's a great idea! It would be great to go on vacation with you!"

With that, the Mings went from a state of confusion to a state of excitement, and they all dug into more of Mindi's colorful salad.

Annoying Summer Songs

The Sunburn Song

(Sing to the tune of "Three Blind Mice.")

Tried to **tan**,
Now I'm burnt.
Here's the thing
That I learnt:
Avoid the glare of those UV rays,
'Cause crackly skin is the
price one pays,
Which leads to crying for
days and days:
"Ouch! That hurts!"

SPF

Is your friend.
Here's what I
Recommend:
The higher numbers
    protect you more,
So read the label
    or you'll be sore.
Unless it's peeling that you adore:
Protect your skin.

Don't skimp **now**,
Use a lot.
Or your flesh
Will be hot.
So cover up from your toes to head,
Or pain'll make you
    wish you were dead,
Plus, like a lobster you'll be bright red,
And boiling . . . mad!

Check, Please

Return to Sender

How to Tell You've Been at Summer Camp Too Long

If you can check off more than four of these sentences, it could be time for you to **check out**.

___ When you refer to your parents, you call them "those **tall people** who sent me here."

___ You no longer **wake up** when you fall out of the top bunk.

___ You've started naming the **flies** in your cabin.

___ You consider any water that's above freezing as "a nice temperature for a **dip**."

___ You wonder whether to **tie your shoes** with a carrick bend, rolling hitch, or cat's-paw.

___ The blisters on your feet look like the camp's **dinner specials**.

___ You actually refer to that narrow, **lumpy thing** you sleep on as a "bed."

___ The mosquitoes have **favorite spots** on your body.

___ You're now **older** than the counselors.

Dish It Out

Banana Dogs

Hot dogs may be a great meal at ballparks. But these **banana dogs** are a great dessert in all parks.

Serves two.

What You Need:

- 1 **adult** (to help)
- 2 navel **oranges**
- 1/2 cup shredded **coconut**
- 1/2 cup miniature **marshmallows**
- 1 tablespoon **honey**
- 2 **bananas**
- 2 **hot dog buns**

What To Do:

1. Ask an adult to **peel the oranges** and slice the sections into bite-size pieces.
2. Place the sliced oranges in a medium-size **mixing bowl**.
3. Add the coconut, marshmallows, and honey to the oranges. **Stir well** and set aside. This is the **topping**.
4. Peel the bananas.
5. Place one banana in each hot dog bun.
6. Spoon the orange topping onto each banana. Your sweet, **gushy** dog is ready to eat.

Pop Quiz

How **well** do you know Nickelodeon's *The Secret World of Alex Mack*™? Take this **trivia test** and find out. Circle the correct answer for each question below. **Answers on p. 127.**

1. Which of the following things can Alex do?
   a. **morph into a liquid**
   b. **become invisible**
   c. **fly**

2. The chemical that gave Alex her secret powers is called:
   a. **BH-90210**
   c. **H_2O**
   b. **GC-161**

3. Which other character on the show has the same powers as Alex?

a. **her dad**

b. **her sister, Annie**

c. **Dave's chimpanzee**

4. In junior high, Alex had a crush on:

a. **her best friend, Ray**

b. **an older guy in school named Scott**

c. **Jonathan Taylor Thomas**

5. To earn money for Christmas presents one year, Alex gets a job as a:

a. **magician**

b. **Christmas-tree salesperson**

c. **race-car mechanic**

6. Alex solves most of her problems:

a. **by becoming invisible**

b. **by writing to "Dear Abby"**

c. **without relying on her secret powers**

Lock Buns

Unscramble the words below to spell out **stuff you wear** in the summer. We did the first one for you.

Answers on p. 127.

snug lasses s u n g l a s s e s

as lands _ _ _ _ _ _ _

sir teeth _ _ _ _ _ _ _ _

lock buns _ _ _ _ _ _ _ _

tap knot _ _ _ _ _ _ _

ten pin tree cells _ _ _ _ _ _

_ _ _ _ _ _ _ _ _ _ _ _ _ _

Scrambles

Animal Actors

Each **animal-related phrase** below is made up of letters from a celebrity's name. Can you **unscramble** the phrases so they correctly complete each star's name? We did the first one for you. **Answers on p. 127.**

~~rat loot~~   **road fish**   **pale eel**

quail shoe   **windy cod**

J O H N   T R A V O L T A

N _ V _   C _ M _ B _ _ _

C _ _ _ _   _ R A _ F _ R _

_ _ A _ _ _ _ L E   _ 'N _ _ L

_ _ R _ _ _ _ O N   _ _ R _

Still More Jokes

Knock, knock.

Who's there?

Illinois.

Illinois who?

He'll annoy you in the car—my brother, that is.

What's it called when you park the car and make your brother or sister get out?

A pest stop.

What's the difference between a dog who sticks his head out of the car window and your brother?

One is a neck in the pane, and the other is a pain in the neck.

When do car wheels get sad?

When their tires are low.

Why couldn't the tire quit his job?

He was flat broke.

Why did the kid throw quarters under the car wheel?

He wanted to help change a tire.

Why do good bowlers never worry about flat tires?

Because they always pick up a spare.

What goes best with toast when you're in an RV?

Traffic jam.

What's the first thing Frankenstein's monster does when he gets in the car?

He fastens his seat bolts.

Backseat Business

Venus de Smile-O

Are you **bored stiff** in the backseat? Then it's time to play Venus de Smile-O!

The object of the game is to keep a **straight face**—a face as stiff as a statue—while your opponent does everything in his or her power to make you **laugh**.

What You Need:

- At least two **people**
- A **watch** (or someone to tell you when three minutes have passed)

How to Play:

1. One person is the **Statue**. The other player is called **Leonardo**.
2. To start the game, Leonardo calls out **"Freeze!"** The Statue must then freeze, no matter what she was doing—staring, yawning, or picking her nose.
3. Leonardo then has three minutes to make the Statue **smile**. Leonardo can make faces, draw goofy pictures, act out funny scenes, or even imitate the Statue. He can do anything for a laugh—except touch the Statue, talk, or make any noises with his mouth.
4. The round is over as soon as the Statue or Leonardo laughs, or if **three minutes** go by without the Statue cracking a smile. Then the two players switch roles.

Scoring:

- If the Statue laughs:
  Ten points for Leonardo
- If Leonardo cracks up:
  Ten points for the Statue
- If the Statue doesn't smile after three minutes:
  Ten points for the Statue
- If uncontrollable fits of laughter result in an adult turning the car around and canceling the vacation:
  Game over. Laughing kid is crowned Season Champ.

Dear ____________
(parent)

Ask a **friend** or family member to give you the words to **fill in the blanks** below. Then read this letter **out loud**.

Hi, Mom and Dad!

Boy, am I ____________ that
(adjective)

you sent me here to Camp Muck-A-

____________. I've never had
(item of clothing)

such a(n) ____________ time!
(adjective)

Each day we are awoken at

_______________ by the _______________
(number under five) (-ing verb)

of the camp ____________________, Duke.
(animal)

We roll out of our ____________________
(plural noun)

and put on ____________________ layers
(large number)

of clothing—it gets darn _______________
(adjective)

here in the morning! Then we have to

jump in the ____________________ to earn
(noun)

a Polar Bear Club badge. If your lips turn

____________________, you don't get a
(color)

badge, and you have to spend a week

washing the camp's ____________________.
(plural noun)

Bummer!

Yesterday morning my lips managed to

stay red, but my ____________________
(body part)

turned ________________! So I decided
(color)

to _________________ the rest of the day
(verb)

in my ____________________. By four
(noun)

o'clock, the swelling had gone down and I

could return to color wars, though my team

lost ______________ to ______________.
(large number) (tiny number)

Tomorrow I'm going to try for a badge

again, but first I'm going to coat myself in

a thick layer of ____________________. I'm
(gooey substance)

sure that'll do it.

Love,

____
(your name)

The Missing Beetle Mystery

Shelby Woo, the main character of Nickelodeon's *The Mystery Files of Shelby Woo*™, is a 16-year-old high-school student—and an amateur detective. When she's not helping her grandfather run his bed-and-breakfast, she works as an intern at the local police station, where she often helps crack their toughest cases. Can you solve this short mystery along with Shelby?

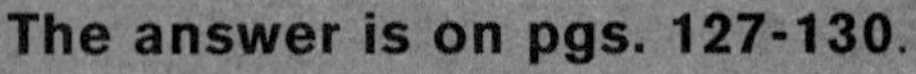
The answer is on pgs. 127-130.

"Someone walked off with an ancient Egyptian scarab today."

Shelby Woo turned up the radio. She was supposed to be mopping the kitchen floor of her grandfather's bed-and-breakfast, but news of a crime was too hard to resist.

"*It was a daring theft,*" the news announcer continued, "*right in the middle of the Cocoa Beach Art Museum. The ancient piece of jewelry was on display in an open case. Sometime between two-thirty and three in the afternoon, the beetle-shaped artifact disappeared. Police are still scrambling to explain how the robbery could have taken place. The only clue is some blue threads that were caught on the edge of the display case.*"

"An Egyptian scarab?" Shelby repeated. "Who would steal an Egyptian scarab?"

"Maybe someone who likes bugs," said Mike Woo, Shelby's grandfather and the owner of the inn where they both lived.

"Grandpa!" Shelby scolded him. "This is serious! The art museum is only a few miles from here."

"And you're going to solve the crime, of course," Mr. Woo replied with a smile. He scratched his head. "Didn't one of our guests, Sandra Clay, say she was a professor of Egyptian history? She would know about scarabs."

"Yes, I am an Egyptologist," said a tall, blond woman with pale skin and blue eyes, who was now standing in the kitchen doorway. She wore a sleeveless blue sundress over a red bathing suit. On her shoulder she carried a straw beach bag.

"Hi, Professor Clay," Mr. Woo said. "Shelby is very excited about the stolen scarab." He told her the news.

"That's terrible. It must have happened when I was at the beach," the professor said.

"Are scarabs valuable?" Shelby asked. "Who would steal one?"

"There are collectors who would give thousands of dollars for an artifact from ancient Egypt," the professor answered.

"Really?" Shelby looked at the Egyptologist carefully. "Do you collect artifacts yourself?"

Sandra laughed. "Yes, but I don't steal my specimens. Besides, I was at the beach all day."

"If you were at the beach all day, why don't you have a tan?" Shelby asked.

Her grandfather gave her a stern look. "Shelby," he said, "I told you to stop treating all our guests as suspects."

Sandra laughed again. "That's alright, Mr. Woo," she said good-naturedly. "As a scientist, I respect an analytical mind. The answer is I always carry a big tube of sunblock right here."

She patted her beach bag.

Shelby looked embarrassed. "Sorry, Professor Clay," she apologized. Just then, a loud man's voice could be heard from the front hall.

"Hello? Is anyone here?"

"We're in here, Mr. Oster!" Shelby's grandfather answered. A moment later, a tall man with a round, red face joined them in the kitchen. Marty Oster was another guest at the bed-and-breakfast. As he entered the room, he held up a blue jacket.

"Hi, Professor Clay, Mr. Woo, Shelby," he said pleasantly. "Do you have a needle and thread? I seem to have torn the sleeve on my jacket."

"Did you hear the news?" Shelby asked. She

told him about the stolen scarab.

"I don't believe it!" Marty shouted. "I must have been there when it happened."

"You went to the museum again today?" Shelby asked. He seemed to be spending his whole vacation visiting the art museum.

"Yes," Marty replied. He looked embarrassed. "I wanted to see the exhibit on ancient Egypt one more time. Have I ever told you I've always been fascinated with pharaohs, and pyramids, and mummies, and—"

"Yes, I think you've mentioned it a few times already," Shelby replied. Marty was always talking about it. "So you were there when the scarab was stolen?" she asked.

"I guess so," he said slowly. "I was there until two-thirty. I wanted to get to Barnacle Bob's before they closed at three. I love their seafood sandwich."

"Well, this is very interesting, but I have to change," said Sandra. As she walked to the door,

she tried to squeeze past Marty, but he stumbled as he stepped backward. He grabbed for something to keep from falling, and his hand caught on Sandra's straw bag. With a clatter, the beach bag and Marty's jacket fell to the floor.

"You idiot!" Sandra cried. Shelby looked down. Everything that had been inside the bag and the jacket was scattered over the kitchen tiles. There was a towel, sunglasses, a magazine, some keys, and a wrapper from Barnacle Bob's with a half-eaten sandwich in it. And right in the middle of the pile was a gem-encrusted piece of jewelry shaped like a beetle.

"That beetle!" Shelby cried. "Is it—?"

"The scarab!" Sandra gasped. "I recognize it." She pointed her finger at Marty. "It was in your jacket. You stole it! Quick, call the police!"

"Me?" Marty shouted. "It wasn't me! It must have been in your bag! You're the thief!"

Shelby knelt down and scooped up the ancient artifact. "Grandpa, you better call

Detective Hineline. Tell him we have the stolen scarab—and the crook."

"Sure, Shelby," Mr. Woo replied. "But which one's the crook?"

Shelby **knows** who stole the Egyptian scarab.
Do **you**?

When you're ready for the solution, turn to p. 127.

Pop Quiz

How **well** do you know Nickelodeon's *The Angry Beavers*™? Take this **trivia test** and find out. Circle true or false next to each statement. **Answers on p. 130.**

T F 1. Daggett is older than Norbert.

T F 2. In Scandinavian, Norbert means "brilliant hero."

T F 3. Daggett and Norbert have to move out of their parents' house when their new siblings are born.

T F 4. The Beavers have a bunk-bed set made out of huge bongo drums.

T F 5. The Beavers live in fear of the Spleen With an Opposable Thumb.

T F 6. Norbert's case of Stinky Toe, a rare beaver disease, is cured when he rubs his toe with grape jelly.

T F 7. SPOOT, the name of the company that tries to find a cure for Stinky Toe, stands for Stinky Poo Technologies.

T F 8. Bing is the name of a beaver whose teeth are so long, he can't close his mouth.

T F 9. The Goode family adopts Norbert and Daggett as pets until the beavers eat the Goode Leg, a wooden family heirloom.

T F 10. The Beavers often try to pass themselves off as weasels.

T F 11. The Beavers are allergic to jalapeño peppers.

Parental Guidance

Bedtime Bluffing

Next time your parents insist it's time to go to sleep, follow these steps and make your dream of **staying up late** come true.

Wear **plastic fangs** and confess that you're a vampire.

Show them *Nightmare on Elm Street* and ask, "Do you want that to happen to **me**?"

Explain that the country is now on Daylight *Super* Savings Time, so it's actually only **four in the afternoon**.

Tell them your science teacher assigned you to look for **shooting stars**.

Insist you must **stand guard** through the night, in case of a Viking attack.

Laugh and say, "I'm already in bed. You're just **dreaming** that I'm still up!"

Wear your pajamas when you watch TV at night. When your parents try to send you to bed, say "I can't hear you. I'm **sleep-watching**."

Explain that you have to stay up until **midnight** because you're practicing for New Year's Eve.

Annoying Summer Songs

Lost in the Forest

(Sing to the tune of "She'll Be Coming 'Round the Mountain.")

We are **lost** in the forest,
yes we are (yes we are).
We are not where we started,
we've gone far (we've gone far).
All the trails seem so familiar,
And the trees are rather similar,
We are lost in the forest,
yes we are (yes we are).

And we **don't** have a compass,
it's at home (it's at home).
So without its trusty pointer
we must roam (we must roam).
It would really come in handy,

Knowing north from south is dandy,
But we don't have a compass,
it's at home (it's at home).

And we **all** blame each other,
yes we do (yes we do).
As arrival at our camp
is overdue (overdue).
We point at the other guy,
Then we sit on leaves and cry,
And we all blame each other,
yes we do (yes we do).

And at **last** the rescue party
comes along (comes along).
They were attracted by our loud
annoying song (annoying song).
To the campsite we will run,
Our long hike is nearly done,
For at last the rescue party's
come along (come along).

Scrambles Goat Bin

Unscramble the words below to spell out names of **things people do in the summer.** We did the first one for you. **Answers on p. 130**.

fig shin f i s h i n g

blab sale _ _ _ _ _ _ _ _

long sinker _ _ _ _ _ _ _ _ _ _

broke tacks _ _ _ _ _ _ _ _ _ _

goat bin _ _ _ _ _ _ _

lovely ball _ _ _ _ _ _ _ _ _ _

kites groan bad

_ _ _ _ _ _ _ _ _ _ _ _ _

Total Tongue Tie-ups

Can you say these **tongue twisters** ten times, fast?

A highly happy Haley hollered "Hallelujah!"

My friends Fred, Frank, and Frieda were flicking icky fleas and ticks off the furry face of Fido.

The sun's great gleam gave Glen's goggles a glorious glow.

When Ron watches reruns, Juan really wonders why.

Pop Quiz

How **well** do you know Nickelodeon's *The Mystery Files of Shelby Woo*™? Take this **trivia test** and find out. Circle the correct answer for each question below. **Answers on p. 130.**

1. Shelby's best friends, Cindi and Noah, work at:
   a. **the police station**
   b. **a photo shop**
   c. **C.J.'s Burger Joint**

2. Shelby leads the audience through each episode with:

a. **her computer**

b. **her diary and some instant photographs**

c. **a VCR hooked up to her brain**

3. Shelby's grandfather, Mike Woo, used to:

a. **be a karate teacher**

b. **work for the San Francisco police**

c. **own a coffee shop**

4. Shelby's friend Noah hopes to one day:

a. **become a detective**

b. **work as an actor**

c. **build an ark**

5. In real life, Irene Ng, who plays Shelby:

a. **is a student at Harvard University**

b. **is a private detective in Los Angeles**

c. **runs a fast-food restaurant called Woo-Woo's**

Jokes Again

Why did Superman carry a rod and reel into the air?

He wanted to try fly-fishing.

❋

What did the fish say to the fisherman?

"I'll see you reel soon."

❋

What do fishermen say on Halloween?

"Trick or trout."

❋

What sport do fish like best?

Bass-ketball.

❋

How long did it take the fish to develop a taste for worms?

One bite and he was hooked.

How did Sam get into the bait business?

He wormed his way in.

*

How did the log do on his first day at camp?

He got fired.

*

What did he say next?

"Looks like I've met my match."

What do you call a newlywed walking in the woods?

A hitched hiker.

*

What do you call campers who don't know how to eat toasted marshmallows with chocolate bars on graham crackers?

S'morons.

Scrambles

Eat These Words

Each **food-related phrase** below is made up of letters from a celebrity's name. Can you **unscramble** the phrases so they correctly complete each star's name? We did the first one for you. **Answers on p. 130.**

~~cereal~~ nose rye corn head

cake hot jam on toast

L A **C** **E** Y C H **A** B **E** **R** T

R I _ K I L _ _ _

M I _ _ A _ L J _ _ _ _ _

J A _ _ _ _ _ M _ U _

_ _ N A _ _ _ _ _ _ Y L _ R

_ H _ _ A _

Green Slime™ Frankenstein

You won't blink an **eyeball** at this green-slime cake. It's **monstrously** delicious.

Serves at least six.

What You Need:

For the Cake:

- 1 **adult** (to help)
- 1 store-bought **pound cake**

- 1 pint vanilla **ice cream** (slightly softened)
- 1 pint ice cream in **any flavor you want** (slightly softened)
- 1/2 cup **chocolate chips**
- 1/2 cup **chopped nuts** (optional)

For the Green Slime Icing:

- 1 cup **whipping cream**
- 1/2 teaspoon **vanilla**
- 2 tablespoons **sugar**
- 3 or 4 drops **green food coloring**

For Decoration:

- 1/4 cup **chocolate chips**
- 1/4 cup **chopped nuts** (optional)
- 2 to 4 **grapes**
- 2 black **licorice** strips

- 1 sheet **waxed paper**, about 24 inches long
- 1 sheet **aluminum foil**, about 24 inches long

What To Do:

1. Ask an adult to **slice off** the top third of the pound cake and then the next third, so you have **3 long slabs** of cake.
2. Place the bottom slice of cake on the waxed paper.
3. Spread as much of the **vanilla ice cream** as you want over the top of the slice, covering it completely.
4. Sprinkle 1/4 cup chocolate chips and 1/4 cup chopped nuts **over the ice cream**.
5. Place the second slice of cake on top.
6. Spread as much of the other flavor of ice cream as you want over the top of the slice, covering it completely.
7. Sprinkle 1/4 cup chocolate chips and 1/4 cup chopped nuts over the ice cream.
8. Place the third slice of cake on top.
9. **Wrap the entire cake** tightly in the waxed paper. Then wrap the cake in the aluminum foil.

continued

10. Put the cake in the **freezer** for 2 hours.
11. Just before you're ready to take the cake out of the freezer, pour the **whipping cream** into a mixing bowl. Stir in the sugar, vanilla, and food coloring.
12. Ask an adult to help you whip the cream mixture until **soft peaks** form.
13. Take the cake out of the freezer, unwrap it, and place it on a plate. **Spread the green slime** icing all over the cake with a spatula.
14. Decorate the cake to look like a **monster's head**. Push in 2 grapes for eyes. Arrange chocolate chips in a line to look like a **scar**, or use them for a nose or **hair**. Use 1 black licorice strip for the eyebrows and the other one for a mouth. Sprinkle chopped nuts all over. **Poke** a whole grape into either side of the monster's neck, for **bolts**. Or come up with your own monstrous ideas.
15. Ask an adult to help you slice and serve the cake.

Fill-ins

Greetings From

____
(place)

Ask a **friend** or family member to give you the words to **fill in the blanks** below. Then read this letter **out loud**.

YOU'RE SURE TO GET YOUR **FILL** OF

____________________ AT UNCLE JOHN'S
(plural noun)

____________________ HOUSE!
(noun)

YOU **KILL** 'EM, WE **GRILL** 'EM!

Dear ________________________,
(your friend's name)

Having ______________________. Wish
(noun)

you were here! Today we drove

________________________ miles and only
(really big number)

stopped twice. I started to get tired of

________________________ my brother so I
(-ing verb)

________________________ a book for a while.
(past tense verb)

That put me to sleep for several hours.

When I woke up, we were still in

________________________! Imagine my
(boring state)

surprise.

Later on, we stopped at the diner on

this card, and I had some deep-fried

________________________ and a side order of
(plural noun)

__________________ with salsa. Then
(food)

we stopped at a __________________
(noun)

station for some __________________
(liquid)

for the car, and my dad let me fill up the

__________________. That was the most
(noun)

fun I've had in __________________.
(amount of time)

Tonight we'll be camping at the Big

__________________ National Park. Too
(noun)

bad we forgot the tent!

See you soon,

____
(your name)

Answers

Scrambles: Pie Cop (page 5):

eat dice = iced tea; her best = sherbet; lone dame = lemonade; race mice = ice cream; raging eel = ginger ale; hi to some = smoothie.

Pop Quiz: *KABLAM!* (pages 6-7):

1-t; 2-f; 3-t; 4-f; 5-f; 6-t; 7-f; 8-f; 9-f; 10-t; 11-f; 12-t; 13-f.

Pop Quiz: *All That* (pages 20-21):

1-a; 2-b; 3-a; 4-a; 5-c; 6-b; 7-a.

Scrambles: Did I Get the Part? (page 22):

eyes = Mike Myers; liver stone = Oliver Stone; leg hop = Whoopi Goldberg; music toe = Tom Cruise.

Passport Pups (pages 29-33):

home; Apple; flamingo; Andes; equator; Tower; gondola; Pyramid; safari; furry; pet; China; over.

Pop Quiz: ***Hey Arnold!*** (pages 34-35):

1-f; 2-f; 3-t; 4-f; 5-t; 6-f; 7-f; 8-t; 9-t; 10-f; 11-t; 12-f; 13-t; 14-f; 15-t.

Pop Quiz: ***Kenan & Kel*** (pages 50-51):

1-c; 2-a; 3-b; 4-a; 5-c; 6-b.

Pop Quiz: ***AAAHH!!! Real Monsters*** (pages 64-65):

1-t; 2-f; 3-f; 4-f; 5-t; 6-t; 7-t; 8-f; 9-t; 10-t.

The State of Mings (pages 68-77):

Shiloh, I ought = Ohio

Gore-Tex as an excuse = Texas

already washing tons of = Washington

radio wailing = Iowa

Mindi, an A student = Indiana

a gala skating party = Alaska

a rut, a huge rut = Utah

my new jersey = New Jersey

lemon, tan almonds = Montana

florid, as usual = Florida

Ken, tuck your shirt = Kentucky

Lou is. I analyzed = Louisiana

Ferrari Z on an = Arizona

Virgin. I always = Virginia

west. Virgin! I am = West Virginia

miss our incredibly = Missouri

north. Carol in a car = North Carolina

south, Carol in a car = South Carolina

bark. An S.A.S. = Arkansas

shock—an S.A.S. = Kansas

miss. Is sipping tea = Mississippi

Ma in England = Maine

said. "A hotel room = Idaho

Mary. Land is = Maryland

north—Dako! Take = North Dakota

south. . . . Dako! Take = South Dakota

said Al. "A *bam* always = Alabama

put a color ad on the table = Colorado

new. Yo, RKO = New York

drive over. Monty's = Vermont

extra large, or giant size = Georgia

"Catarrh Ode" is landing = Rhode Island

rottenness. Eesh!" = Tennessee

Can you get it, Min? Nesota = Minnesota

in, Eva, darling. = Nevada

ill? I noisily banged = Illinois

hardly knew me, X. I couldn't = New Mexico

"Wow! Is Con singing = Wisconsin

dewy. "O Ming family = Wyoming

Pop Quiz: *The Secret World of Alex Mack* (pages 84-85):

1-a; 2-b; 3-c; 4-b; 5-b; 6-c.

Scrambles: Lock Buns (page 86):

as lands = sandals; sir teeth = tee shirt; lock buns = sunblock; tap knot = tank top; ten pin tree cells = insect repellent.

Scrambles: Animal Actors (page 87):

pale eel = Neve Campbell; windy cod = Cindy Crawford; quail shoe = Shaquille O'Neal; road fish = Harrison Ford.

The Missing Beetle Mystery (pages 96-103):

Shelby looked from Marty to Sandra. "Well," she said thoughtfully, "both of you have a motive to steal the scarab. Professor Clay, you could

add it to your private collection. And Mr. Oster, you've always been fascinated with ancient Egypt. Maybe you'd like to start a collection of your own."

"I would never steal a scarab!" Marty protested.

"Maybe," Shelby replied. "Except you admit you were at the art museum this afternoon. And you have a torn blue jacket. The police found blue threads on the display case."

"That proves it!" Sandra cried. "His sleeve must have ripped when he stole the scarab."

"Yes, it could have been," Shelby continued. "Except for one thing. Mr. Oster was at Barnacle Bob's today—this half a sandwich is still fresh. Barnacle Bob's always closes at three, because Bob likes to go fishing. The scarab was stolen between two-thirty and three o'clock. So Mr. Oster couldn't have taken it." Shelby paused. "But you could have done it, Professor Clay," she said, nodding her head. "You're wearing a

blue dress."

"But I told you," Sandra said. "I was at the beach all day."

"Yes, with your sunblock," Shelby answered. "Except there was no sunblock in your bag!" she said, pointing to the beach bag's contents, still lying on the floor. "If you were at the beach, like you say, you'd be as red as a lobster now without any sunblock! The scarab must have fallen out of your bag!"

Sandra looked from Shelby to Mr. Woo to Marty. She opened her mouth as if to say something. Then suddenly she turned and dashed for the kitchen door. But Marty and Mr. Woo got there first.

"You'd better hang around, Professor Clay," Shelby's grandfather said calmly but firmly. "The police will want to talk to you."

Later, when Detective Hineline had led Sandra Clay to jail, Mike Woo congratulated his granddaughter.

"You did it again, Shelby," he smiled. "And I know one thing I'll do the next time I see a beetle on our kitchen floor."

"What's that, Grandpa?"

"Call an exterminator," he said with a grin.

Pop Quiz: *The Angry Beavers*

(pages 104-105):

1-f; 2-t; 3-t; 4-f; 5-t; 6-f; 7-t; 8-f; 9-t; 10-f; 11-f.

Scrambles: Goat Bin (page 110):

blab sale = baseball; long sinker = snorkeling; broke tacks = backstroke; goat bin = boating; lovely ball = volleyball; kites groan bad = skateboarding.

Pop Quiz: *The Mystery Files of Shelby Woo*

(pages 112-113):

1-b; 2-a; 3-b; 4-b; 5-a.

Scrambles: Eat These Words (page 116):

cake = Ricki Lake; corn head = Michael Jordan; nose rye = Jane Seymour; hot jam on toast = Jonathan Taylor Thomas.

NICKELODEON/MINSTREL BOOKS POINTS PROGRAM

Official Rules

1. *HOW TO COLLECT POINTS*

Points may be collected by purchasing any book with the special Minstrel®/Nickelodeon "Read Books, Earn Points, Get Stuff!" offer. Only books that bear the burst "Read Books, Earn Points, Get Stuff!" are eligible for the program. Points can be redeemed for merchandise by completing the coupons (found in the back of the books) and mailing with a check or money order in the exact amount to cover postage and handling to Minstrel Books/Nickelodeon Points Program, P.O. Box 7777-G140, Mt. Prospect, IL 60056-7777. Each coupon is worth points. (See individual book for point value.) Copies of coupons are not valid. Simon & Schuster is not responsible for lost, late, illegible, incomplete, stolen, postage-due, or misdirected mail.

2. *40 POINT MINIMUM*

Each redemption request must contain a minimum of 40 points in order to redeem for merchandise.

3. *ELIGIBILITY*

Open to legal residents of the United States (excluding Puerto Rico) and Canada (excluding Quebec) only. Void where taxed, licensed, restricted, or prohibited by law. Redemption requests from groups, clubs, or organizations will not be honored.

4. *DELIVERY*

Allow 6-8 weeks for delivery of merchandise.

5. *MERCHANDISE*

All merchandise is subject to availability and may be replaced with an item of merchandise of equal or greater value at the sole discretion of Simon & Schuster.

6. *ORDER DEADLINE*

All redemption requests must be received by January 31, 1999, or while supplies last. Offer may not be combined with any other promotional offer from Simon & Schuster. Employees and the immediate family members of such employees of Simon & Schuster, its parent company, subsidiaries, divisions and related companies and their respective agencies and agents are ineligible to participate.

COMPLETE THE COUPON AND MAIL TO
NICKELODEON/MINSTREL POINTS PROGRAM
P.O. BOX 7777-G140
MT. PROSPECT, IL 60056-7777

NICKELODEON®
MINSTREL® BOOKS

NAME ______________________________

ADDRESS ______________________________

CITY ______________________________ STATE _____ ZIP ______

THIS COUPON WORTH FIVE POINTS

Offer expires January 31, 1999

I have enclosed _____coupons and a check/money order (in U.S. currency only) made payable to "Nickelodeon/Minstrel Books Points Program" to cover postage and handling.

- ❑ 40–75 points (+ $3.50 postage and handling)
- ❑ 80 points or more (+ $5.50 postage and handling)

1464-01(2of2)

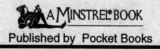